CELTIC DESIGNS

REBECCA MCKILLIP

Stemmer
House
Publishers

A Barbara Holdridge book

First Printing 1981
Second Printing 1984
Third Printing 1988
Fourth Printing 1991
Fifth Printing 1992
Sixth Printing 1995
Seventh Printing 1997
Eight Printing 2000
Ninth Printing 2001
Tenth Printing 2003
Eleventh Printing 2005

Printed and bound in the United States of America

COVER ILLUSTRATION: An adaptation of a design from the Book of Kells, originally
measuring just one-third inch in diameter, it contains four beasts, four
serpents, four birds and four men, with a vine and red berries interwoven.

Introduction

THE EARLIEST PEOPLE KNOWN AS CELTS inhabited a wide geographic area ranging from Spain to southern Scandinavia, and from Hungary to the Atlantic coasts of Ireland. Scattered over this area, these prehistoric peoples shared a common culture, with similar languages, myths, rituals, literature and art. The earliest Celtic art comes from the iron-using prehistoric culture called *Hallstatt,* but the most refined examples of the early style come from the *La Tène* culture, named for artifacts found near a village in Switzerland. Examples of *La Tène* weapons and jewelry date back to at least 2500 B.C.; yet even at this early date the lines and motifs of the designs are distinctly *Celtic.* These early Celts loved ornate decoration, and their artists filled every available space on sword scabbards or clothes fasteners with intricate repeating designs.

By the time of the Roman Conquest of Britain in the first century A.D., the *La Tène* culture was on the decline in continental Europe, but it continued to develop and flourish in the British Isles, especially in Ireland. Ireland remained relatively unaffected by such outside calamities as the fall of the Roman Empire and the Teutonic invasions, and so for nearly nine centuries after the Roman Conquest, the peaceful culture of Ireland provided the perfect atmosphere in which to develop the art of the Celts. What is generally known today as Celtic art is the continuation and ultimate perfection, in Ireland, of the art which began centuries before in the prehistoric *Hallstatt* culture.

The coming of Christianity to Ireland between the fifth and sixth centuries had a profound effect on the development of Celtic art. Prior to this time, there existed in Ireland many small kingdoms which maintained a prickly independence from each other. Men who were called the *aes dana,* skilled in the disciplines of literature, music, law, philosophy, religion, and art, were accorded much respect and lofty positions at the courts. They enjoyed the privilege of being able to travel unmolested from one kingdom to another. Pagan Ireland had developed a highly sophisticated artistic tradition, and Christian missionaries must have recognized and appreciated the value of the pagan Celtic culture. Rather than alienating the pagan culture and disrupting its art, the new religion provided a central belief through which the Irish Celts were united for the first time.

Christian missionaries established monasteries which functioned as cultural and academic centers, as well as spiritual communities. The monastic communities became the new patrons of the arts. These great centers drew the *aes dana*, who were eager to pursue their studies of law, music, poetry and art. At such monasteries as those on the islands of Iona and Lindisfarne, the artist could practice and develop his creativity in the company of skilled and diligent colleagues, in the peaceful atmosphere necessary for intricate work.

Christianity brought new artistic outlets for Celtic craftsmen. The wealth of symbolism of the new religion was inspiration for new kinds of designs. The institutions themselves created a demand for sacred objects such as crosses, chalices, reliquaries (ornate containers for sacred remains), and religious books. All of these things had to be carved, forged, decorated or lettered by the Celtic artisans. The era of early Christianity in Ireland, from about the fifth to the late eighth centuries, has been called the "Golden Age" of Celtic art, although it was not until the mid-seventh century that the truly astonishing masterpieces of the art were created. Little more than a century later, Ireland was invaded by Vikings, whose plundering raids disrupted the progression of this Golden Age.

The unparalled beauty of style and craftsmanship of Celtic art in Ireland can be largely attributed to its unique insular development, but it is true that Celtic artists in Ireland had some contact with the artistic styles of previous and contemporary cultures. They would have seen examples of Mediterranean motifs figured on vessels of imported wine and oil, and traveling Irish monks probably brought back descriptions of carved stone slabs and illuminated manuscripts of other cultures, including those of Syria and Egypt. But even though Celtic artists made use of certain motifs and styles from the art of other culutres, they incorporated them into a unique artistic style which differs significantly from even that of nearby Roman Britain.

Celtic decoration was worked upon a variety of surfaces, ranging from carvings on fifteen-foot slabs of sandstone to the delicate tracery of gold filigree on an ornamental brooch. Today, massive standing slabs of carved stone mark the Irish countryside. Huge decorated crosses were the chief static ornaments of the monasteries, and some are now the only visible remains of these great cultural and spiritual centers. Celtic artists were nothing if not adaptable, and when the Vikings stripped their monasteries bare of the carefully crafted treasures, the Celts began to carve out their designs on chunks of stone too massive to be stolen from them. Examples of Celtic metalwork exist in a relatively large number, probably proportionate to the medium's popularity and durability. The Celts are legendary for their love of gold. They fashioned their weapons, clothes fasteners and jewelry in gold and adorned these objects with sumptuous filigree, enamelwork and gems. The elegant refinement of the Ardagh challice and the delicate filigree of the Tara Brooch are testimony to the superlative skill of the metalsmiths, but this skill can be seen even in the coils of a simple gold button.

Christianity helped to introduce the written word into Celtic literature, which had been an almost exclusively oral tradition up to this point. The new Christian monasteries trained scribes and artists to create copies of the Latin Bible, and the artistic potential of the illuminated manuscript was soon to be realized. Thus the book, the principal tool of a historic civilization, was able to preserve and develop the art of a prehistoric culture.

The earliest existing example of a Celtic illuminated manuscript is the *Cathach of St. Columba,* which is thought to have been completed at the end of the sixth century. It is now just a fragment of the original psalter, or book of the Psalms, and is nicknamed "Battler." This name comes from the legend that generations of the family of Conall Gulban used the book to ensure victory, by carrying it three times around their army before going into battle. Despite Ireland's conversion to Christianity, some of the beliefs of the pagan cults lingered in the mystical significance attributed to the manuscript itself, often to its detriment. A farmer named MacGeoghan, having somehow acquired the Book of Durrow (a gospel book of the latter half of the seventh century), used it to cure his sick cattle by pouring their drinking water over the book. Such unfortunate superstitious practices may partially account for the extremely small number of surviving manuscripts! Historians can only guess at the number of manuscripts which may have been created at the great monastic scriptoria, only to be lost through carelessness, or carried to other parts of the world by looters.

The decoration of the *Cathach* is limited to dots of red around the large capital letters in the text. A century later, in the Book of Durrow, the decoration began to occupy a significant place in the manuscript's design. This book of the four gospels according to Sts. Matthew, Mark, Luke and John has a carefully planned scheme of decoration, which sets the style for later gospel books. Each section begins with a decorated page on the left. This page, packed to its borders with ornament, is called a carpet-page. It may have been inspired by Persian manuscript-illumination or by the patterns of Roman mosaics in Britain. In spite of the sacred nature of the gospel book, the ornament-loving Celtic artists saw nothing wrong with devoting an entire page to pure decoration. They used the format of the carpet-page for some of their most delightful and fascinating designs. Facing the carpet-page is an introductory page with a large initial decorated with spirals and dot-edging. Then, each of the four gospels begins with a full-page portrait of the Evangelist who composed its text. Each Evangelist is depicted either in a stylized human form as a scribe, or in the animal shape of his traditional symbols: St. Matthew is the Man, or Angel, St. Mark the Lion, St. Luke the Ox and St. John the Eagle. Almost every page of the Book of Durrow is bordered by interlaced ribbons of deep green, bright yellow and glowing red. The decorated initials serve as a link between the ornament and the text of the gospels. This is the first example of an attempt by Celtic artists to articulate the words of the gospels by means of decoration.

Later, the ornament in a gospel book becomes a literal *illumination* of the words it decorates. In the Book of Kells, which is perhaps the greatest masterpiece of all existing Celtic manuscripts, the ornament has moved from its relatively inconspicuous position in the *Cathach* to a flamboyance which overwhelms the very text. Even though the organization of the decoration is much more uneven than that of the Book of Durrow, the sumptuous ornament which swirls and weaves across each page of the Book of Kells is the most beautiful and complex of all. On some pages the decoration leaves room for only a few significant initial letters of the text. The combined impact of the ornate initials and the pulsating swirls of decoration expresses the mystical symbolism more powerfully than mere words.

A twelfth-century scholar, Giraldus Cambrensis, wrote after examining an Irish gospel book which may have been the Book of Kells:

> "Examine it carefully, and you will penetrate to the very shrine of art. You will make out intricacies so delicate and subtle, so concise and compact, so full of knots and links, in colors so fresh and vivid, that you might think all of this was the work of an angel, not of a man."

Although scholars and art lovers through the centuries have marveled at the Book of Kells, even this great masterpiece has suffered at the hands of vandals and ignoramuses. According to one account, the book was stolen one night from the church of Kells and was discovered more than two months later, stripped of its gold cover and buried under a sod of earth. Sometime within the last two centuries, a careless binder clipped inches from the book's borders, cutting away a precious part of some of the most magnificent artwork of any Western civilization.

In the Book of Kells, every Celtic design motif has been recreated in figures of sophisticated flamboyance, the superlative form of each motif. Spirals whirl one within another, creating a hypnotic, dizzying motion. Ribbon strands of infinite delicacy are knotted and wound into endless, almost indecipherable patterns. One scholar took up his magnifying glass to count 158 strands of interlace within *a single square inch* of decoration. Even more incredible, each tiny strand is formed by a strip of white, bordered by bands of black on each side, tripling the number of tiny lines. Animals born of some fantastic imagination, as well as those of the barnyard variety, behave with geometric precision in interlace patterns and borders. They twist themselves effortlessly into the shapes of capital letters. Some stroll freely through the text, often obligingly punctuating a sentence or pointing out a word. The Book of Kells has over 400 ornamental capital letters, with no two alike. The list of fascinating details goes on and on.

This book, like most gospel books, is probably the work of a highly trained scriptorium, where a number of pupils worked along with the great masters of the art. The first step in the construction was to lay out the plan of the entire book. Designers spent long hours carefully drawing up the composition of each page. The Celtic artist had to be very skilled in mathematics and geometry. He laid out his design on a modular grid pattern, and then marked it in lightly with brown ink. The complexity of many designs required an artist to work several days just in laying out the underdrawing, but the self-discipline necessary for the work was part of the artist-monk's daily life of devotion to God. Interlace patterns of flawless intricacy are only as remarkable as the simple geometric rules on which they are based. What is truly remarkable about these complicated designs is their originality and the meticulous patience with which they were constructed.

After the lettering of the text came the painters to fill in the decoration. A project of such magnitude and complexity as the Book of Kells must have taken several years to complete. This somewhat explains the uneven quality of the decoration—over a period of time there were artists of varying degrees of skill adding their own touches to the book. Colors and styles vary widely—from subdued monochromes to wild tonal clashes, from monumental grandeur to tiny, whimsical detail.

The Celtic artist had a wealth of motifs from which to choose his designs. His skill in manipulating abstract patterns and geometric shapes was a legacy from the artist of the earlier *La Tène* period. The *La Tène* artist's religious beliefs prohibited any kind of imitation of the works of the deities, such as plants and animals, so he became adept at creating abstract designs. The layout of each decorated area is quite orderly and precise, yet the decoration is aimed at creating a sense of movement, a kind of frozen vitality. The spiral is the primary motif of the art. It is a simple, yet sophisticated adaptation of the most basic motifs of lines and circles. From the spiral come the maze-like designs called *key-patterns* because of their interlocking semi-triangular shapes. Key-patterns are just like spirals, drawn along straight, instead of curved, lines. Interlaced bands or ribbons are a decorative motif common to many cultures also. The repeating knots and loops symbolize continuity, and challenge the eye to disentangle the weave by following each strand simultaneously. However, Celtic artists often destroyed the illusion of endlessly interwoven strands by changing colors within a single strand, and thereby obscuring its course. Interlace is used as a filler ornament because of its convenient adaptability to any space. Dot-edging appears frequently in even the earliest of Celtic illuminated manuscripts. Usually done in red ink, the tiny dots outline initial letters, fill in empty spaces, and decorate interlacing strands. They lend a subtle color to an outlined form.

Zoomorphic ornament, that which is based upon the forms of birds, reptiles and other animals, is probably the most imaginative and amusing form of Celtic ornament. Animals and humans appear most frequently as abstract stylizations when they function as part of the decoration. Zoomorphs are found relatively early in the artistic development of the Celts. The earliest animal is a kind of reptilian dog, with jaws and legs flowing out like ribbons. He is taken from an early German prototype, but he changes gradually into a more doglike creature, with heels, claws, ears and snout. His narrow ribbon of a tongue stretches to impossible lengths, to wind itself into knots around the other interwined beasts.

Zoomorphs usually form part of a border or filler pattern. They are linked to each other in any number of amusing positions; usually the jaws of one beast are clamped tenaciously on the tail or hindquarters of the next, with a riot of knotted limbs in between. The antic contortions of these colorful little beasts add a whimsical touch to even the most serious and restrained compositions, yet some of the zoomorphs do function as representations of religious symbols. The feline zoomorph, the dragon-lion-cat, alternately symbolizes the Lion of Judah, the resurrected Christ, or St. Mark the Evangelist. The motif of the coiling serpent with a tail-like streamer at each eye probably comes from pagan snake-worship, but to the Celtic artist the serpent is more than likely just an extremely adaptable interlacing figure.

After Ireland's conversion to Christianity, man appears more and more frequently in Celtic design. Biblical narratives and symbols require the inclusion of human beings in the illustrations, but men appear just as often as fanciful additions to the ornament, where they behave much the same as the zoomorphs. Amusing little men appear in pairs, bound together by entwined limbs, and each with a firm grip on the other's beard. These "Beardpullers" may be the symbol of marketing, or bartering, used by Celtic tradesmen. In the larger portraits of saints, man is seen as a staring, frozen stylization of the human form. The hypnotic gaze of this being is rather like that of Byzantine icons. Any motion in the composition of these portraits is solely in the whirling folds of the saints' drapery. The Celtic artist did not attempt to portray action; rather, he created his own kinetic energy through the rhythmic motion of his design.

Vegetation is extremely rare in Celtic design until the Christian era, after which it is used sparingly. The typical Irish ornamental foliage is a thick creeper, with a three-lobed leaf, much like a clover leaf. Geometric shapes usually take the place of blossoms on the vines.

The Celts made the vellum for their writing surface out of a special preparation of either calfskin or sheepskin. The surface of the vellum is like suede, and is highly receptive to color. Some of the common pigments used are red lead, yellow orpiment and green verdigris. The prolonged brilliance of the colors, even after centuries of exposure, attests to the skill of the Celts as chemists and craftsmen. There is evidence that the Celtic artists used compasses and rulers to work out their designs; but they accomplished a great deal more than the simple lines and circles that these tools help to form. The Celtic artists worked without the benefit of strong artificial lights, magnifying lenses or other sophisticated tools, but their art is among the most sophisticated, unique and beautiful ever created in the history of mankind.

I wish to acknowledge the work of Mr. George Bain, whose CELTIC ART: THE METHODS OF CONSTRUCTION* was an invaluable aid to me in learning to create Celtic design. I recommend it to anyone interested in studying and mastering the technique of Celtic design. It is a marvelous resource and would be, I imagine, even to an accomplished artist of eighth-century Ireland. I would also like to thank Professor Nancy Dorian of Bryn Mawr College for her very kind help with the writing of this introduction, and for her marvelous course on Celtic civilization, through which I discovered the magic of Celtic art.

REBECCA McKILLIP

* Bain, George. *Celtic Art: The Methods of Construction.* New York: Dover Publications, Inc., 1978

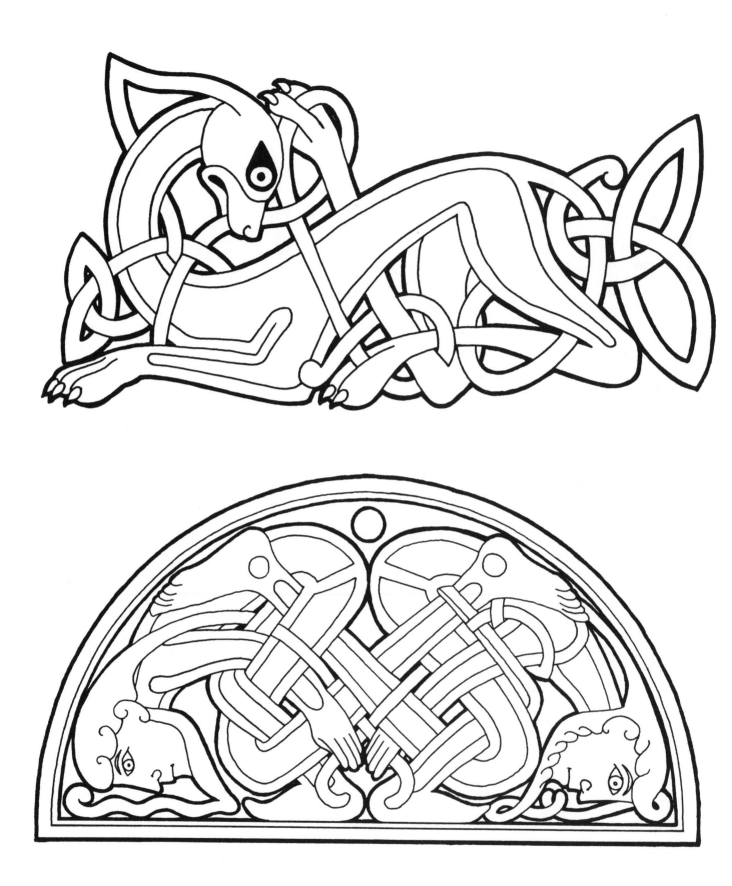

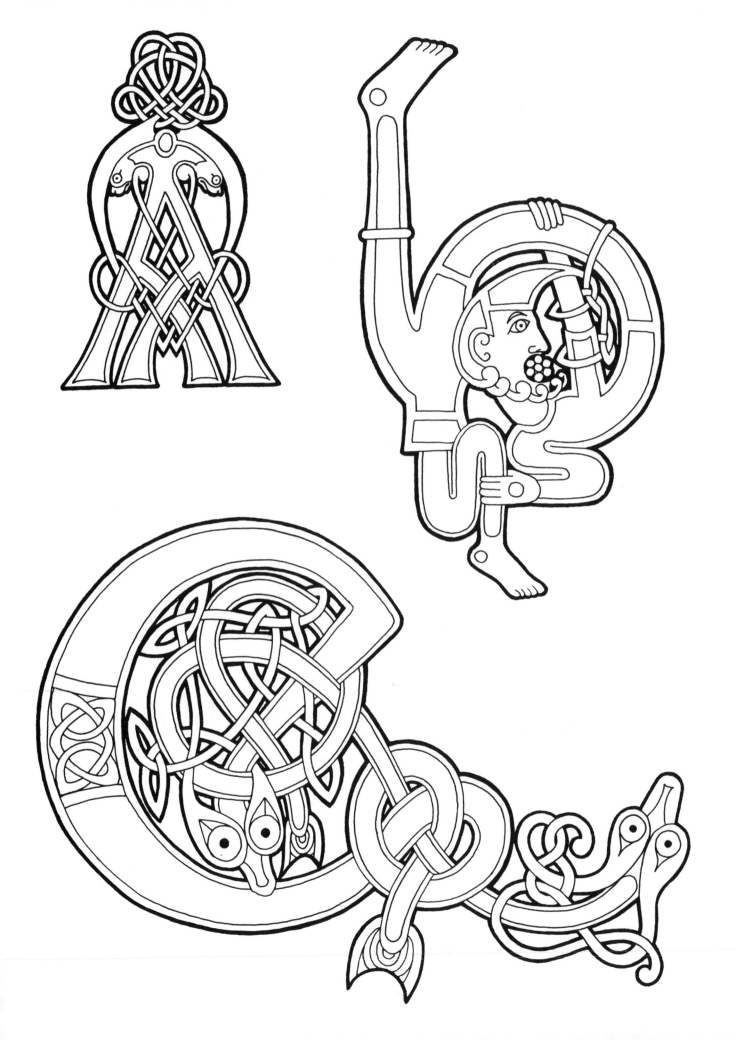

Colophon

Designed by Barbara Holdridge
Composed in Times Roman by
  Brown Composition, Inc.,
  Sparks, Maryland
Cover color separations by
  GraphTec, Annapolis Junction,
  Maryland
Printed on 75-pound Williamsburg
  Return Postcard paper and bound
  by United Graphics, Inc.,
  Mattoon, Illinois